SUCKER

CW00738611

PUNCH

Titles in Between The Lines:

Badger Publishing Limited, Oldmedow Road, Hardwick Industrial Estate, King's Lynn PE30 4JJ

Telephone: 01438 791037

www.badgerlearning.co.uk

SUCKER PUNCH

EMMA NORRY

Badger
LEARNING

Sucker Punch ISBN 978-1-78837-444-6

Publisher / Senior Editor: Danny Pearson
Editor: Claire Wood
Copyeditor: Cheryl Lanyon
Designer: Bigtop Design Ltd
Cover: © Studio 52 film / Alamy Stock Photo

4 6 8 10 9 7 5 3

CHAPTER 1
PRIVATE

Funerals are weird but wakes are weirder. Burying someone is bad enough, but then having a party? It just feels… wrong.

When I first heard the word 'wake', I nearly laughed. Stupid name. The person wasn't awake and never would be again. *Sheesh!* The only person I knew who would also have seen the funny side was Dad. But he wasn't around to share the moment with, seeing as it was *his* wake we were holding.

"Bo, make yourself useful, please," hissed Mum, handing me a plate of limp-looking sandwiches.

Our house was crammed. Dad had been
a friendly guy and, as a plumber, he had a
reputation for honesty, so even though you
wouldn't imagine customers coming to a wake,
loads had turned up.

Aunty Hilda, his sister over from the Caribbean,
was snoozing in my room, so Mum stopped me
from sneaking upstairs, even though all I wanted
to do was hide.

I handed out drinks and sandwiches while people
murmured quietly about how great Dad was and
offered us their sympathies.

Being at the graveside was strange. I didn't
cry. I hope that doesn't sound cold or uncaring.
Of course I was sad. I was *ruined*. I love Dad.
Loved. He wasn't one of those distant,
come-home-late-from-work dads. He made
silly jokes and rarely raised his voice.

When I was ten and obsessed with face-painting,
he let me loose on his face, armed with Mum's
old make-up.

Dad was diagnosed with pancreatic cancer just before my thirteenth birthday. Unfortunately, his symptoms didn't show up until it was far too late, and he died eighteen months later.

Mum blamed herself, even though it wasn't her fault. When he lost weight, she was delighted. She'd been on at him to lose weight for months. When he complained of tummy pain, she rolled her eyes as she handed him indigestion tablets. It was only when he started to look oddly yellow round the edges that we both took his grumbles seriously and sent him off to the doctor.

"Are you alright?" Dad's boss, Judith, asked as I walked past, stinky tuna mayo oozing out of the sandwiches on the plate I held.

She put her hand on my shoulder, squeezing gently.

"Yes, thank you," I replied, politely.

Judith pulled an expression that intended to look sympathetic, but because her eyes went massive and her head suddenly tilted in that zombie-snapped way, she just looked scary.

I headed back into the kitchen and stood at the counter, wrestling with the clingfilm stretched over another plate of sweaty sandwiches.

The loud whispering from the other side of the door sounded like Steve, one of Dad's drinking buddies. I could hear him clearly.

"How come Bo's not crying? That's not normal."

"Steve!" hissed Judith. "Lay off the lager will you? People deal with grief differently. She's probably in shock."

"It can't be shock. Trevor was ill for ages. Keeping it bottled up like that isn't healthy. Not for a fifteen-year-old girl. Well, not for anyone really."

"Shhh!"

Grateful we had two entrances to our kitchen,
I dumped the plate on the worktop and headed
for the toilet.

After I'd locked the door and sat on the closed
seat-lid, I put my head in my hands. Was there
something wrong with me because I wasn't
crying? Did it mean I wasn't sad? That I didn't
love Dad enough?

I wasn't crying because…

… because tears are private, that's why!

No one out there except Mum had any idea what
I was feeling, and I didn't want to hear them all
pretending they did.

I didn't want to hear, "This happened to me too",
or have to nod when they said I'd feel better in
time, or even how much this totally sucked.
I *knew* it sucked.

I didn't want people saying how funny he was,
nor how much he loved me. They didn't know

him better than I did. I was the only person who knew how much he enjoyed picking dirt out of his fingernails with toothpicks when he thought no one was looking.

I didn't want people trying to make me feel better. I didn't want to feel better.

My throat tightened and closed up as if someone had their hands round my neck. My chest started heaving. My eyes prickled and then tears were running down my cheeks. I put my hand over my mouth — I was making quite a noise.

If I didn't stop crying soon, I might not be able to stop.

Get a grip!

Taking a deep, shaking breath, I sniffed loudly and blew my nose. No point in crying now. What good would that do? Tears wouldn't bring him back.

I just wanted everyone except Mum to leave. To get out of our house. It was too loud. If it wasn't noisy because Dad was talking to the TV, or singing Caribbean songs out of tune while pretending to be a Jamaican superstar, then I didn't want any noise at all.

*

That night, sobbing woke me up. I peered at the glow-in-the-dark hands on my alarm clock: 1am.

Mum's room was empty. I leant over the bannister, listening, biting my lip. Mum had never been a big crier, but in the past year all she'd done was cry.

I listened for a long time. I couldn't let her cry alone.

She was curled up in Dad's squashy armchair with a box of tissues in her lap. The TV was turned down low; the boxing on. Obviously she hadn't cancelled the Sports Package yet.

"It's the Anthony Joshua fight," she sniffed. "Trev would have loved this. Though why he enjoyed watching grown men hit each other is beyond my understanding." Her used, soggy tissues were lined up along one armrest like the world's saddest soldiers.

I perched on the other armrest.

Dad never played much sport, but loved watching it. Although I barely understood the rules of his favourites — cricket and American football — I loved how excited he'd get when the boxing was on. He'd jump up and down in his seat and throw a few punches on the cushions.

His favourite boxer was Muhammad Ali. He always said Muhammad Ali wasn't only a boxer, but a man with great morals, as well as being a poet.

"Yeah. Dad would have loved this, wouldn't he?" I said, snuggling next to her. She hugged me close and kissed the top of my head.

We sat there like that for a while.

A few years ago, Dad and I camped out in the living room to watch the Olympics. He even let me miss some school. When Nicola Adams won the gold medal, the first female boxer to win an Olympic title, Dad picked me up and whirled me round. It was one of the best times we ever had.

I hadn't seen any women fight before and, being so young, I wasn't that interested. But seeing how strong and brave Nicola had been was inspirational. Dad started calling me by her nickname, 'babyface', and watching boxing together became our thing.

"It's not about the hitting," I said to Mum now, remembering how Dad had explained it when I'd asked him why he enjoyed it so much. "Professional boxing is like… dancing. It's really graceful. The good ones bob and weave to avoid getting hit at all. It's sort of beautiful. I totally get why Dad loved it."

Dad liked to say I'd have made a good fighter. I'd never looked into it because I was more into athletics, but I hadn't done much this year because of him being so ill. I quit all my after-school clubs because I wanted to be around as much as possible, even though he'd insisted I shouldn't.

But now? Now… maybe boxing *was* something I could do?

CHAPTER 2
HANDS OF STONE

A month after the wake, I found myself outside a gym. Hands of Stone was a long, low building with the entire front made up of windows, so I had a good view without needing to go inside.

I stared through the glass, pretending to read the adverts. This gym was close to home, right on the high street, between a barber's and a chip shop. It was the two-week Easter holidays so, without school getting in the way, maybe now was a good opportunity for me to learn how to box.

Mum wasn't home much these days anyway.

Her friends had suggested she keep herself busy by signing up for different evening classes. If I focused my energy on something else, too, maybe that could be a good distraction. Besides, every little thing wound me up these days. Having an outlet would be cool.

Apart from the school sports hall I'd never set foot in a gym, but I stepped inside anyway. Nothing ventured, nothing gained, Dad liked to say.

Inside on my left was a shop area selling gym gear. Rows of gloves hung from the wall. The other part of the gym was full of punchbags swinging from the ceiling, and there was a small boxing ring at the back. A couple of boys were sparring.

A young woman with a nose piercing and short, bleached-blonde hair sat behind a desk, punching the buttons on a cash register. She glanced up and smiled brightly, which made me feel at ease.

"Hi, can I help?"

"Do you give boxing lessons?" I asked.

"We do! Do you want to fight? Spar? Boxing fitness? Kickboxing?"

"I want to do real boxing. I mean, with the gloves and everything, but don't know where to start."

"Well, you've come in at a good time. We're about to start another under-eighteens training programme. You train for free for six weeks and then the charity match is in June."

"You train us for free?"

She laughed. "We ask you to raise sponsorship money of at least £200, but six weeks is plenty of time to do that. You'll need your own mouthguard and gloves, but we lend you the headgear."

Perfect!

"And when's the training?" I asked.

"Monday, Wednesday and Friday."

Lots of my mates were being awkward around me, not knowing what to say, or if to talk about Dad at all. Being busy three nights a week, instead of making excuses not to go out with them, seemed exactly the distraction I needed.

"What's the charity?"

"MacMillan Cancer Support," said the young woman.

Oh! That settled it.

"First class is 7pm tonight."

"How do I sign up?"

She grinned and pulled out a form from her desk. "I'm Lucy. Let's get sorted then. We'll fill out your contact details and health and safety info. You'll need to return the form tonight with parental consent. Red or blue gloves?" she asked.

I pointed to a pair of red gloves on the wall. Red had been Dad's favourite colour.

"They're £25." She went over to the wall and unhooked them with a long stick. "They're fine for beginners."

*

At ten to seven, I pushed open the gym door. A wave of sweat and heat hit me. Men muttered "Excuse me" as they filed out from their class.

Once inside, I counted thirteen teens waiting, some younger and some older than me. So this was who I'd be training with.

Lucy explained that for the actual match we'd fight three rounds, each lasting one and a half minutes. There'd be a one-minute rest between each round. Regular boxing matches — the ones Dad and I watched — were three minutes per round and could last as long as twelve rounds. They'd scaled this down for beginners.

"Hi!" Lucy said. "Nice to see you back."

I smiled at her, thankful she was making me feel so welcome.

"Hi, everyone! No need to be nervous." She addressed all of us. "We're in this together, raising money for a good cause."

The group of us checked each other out, trying not to be too obvious. I didn't recognise anyone from school. Maybe I'd make some new friends. It had been ages since I'd met new people. Dad's illness and a social life didn't exactly fit together.

Lucy clapped her hands. "First, I'll explain about wrapping your hands and wrists to support and protect them. After a 15-minute warm-up, the trainers will put you into two groups. Red or blue. They'll demonstrate the different punches and then let you loose on the bags if we get time."

She unrolled a strip of long, yellow material that looked a bit like bandages. These were the hand wraps. She explained how to hook the loop over our thumb, and then wrap the length round and round, covering our knuckles and wrists. This lessened the chances of injury. We copied her. It was quite relaxing, once I'd stopped getting tangled up.

A girl who looked younger than me wrapped her hands quickly, talking and laughing with her friend as she did it. She looked so accomplished. I wanted to be like that one day.

After Lucy's warm-up of jogging, push-ups (I had to go on my knees), star jumps and skipping, it took me a while to get my breath back. It felt good though, and I wasn't the only one breathing hard. A tall, skinny girl and I exchanged a grin.

We were split into two groups and told to wait by the punching bags, and that one of the trainers would be with us shortly.

I was in a group of five: three boys and a short girl with glasses. I went over to where I'd left my bag and pulled my bottle of water out.

"I'm James."

"Uh-huh," I grunted, too busy trying to get the lid off my bottle to smile at whoever thought chatting me up here was appropriate.

I had a long drink and then went over to one of the hanging bags and threw a punch to see how it felt.

"Hold it!" The boy who'd called himself James laughed and steadied the bag to a stop. "You'll hurt yourself if you punch without your gloves like that. I'm your trainer. Wait and I'll show you all the proper technique, as a group."

"You're our trainer?" He had a baby face, bright blue eyes and was very short. "Really?"

I must have sounded scornful because he blushed. "I've been coming here for four years. I'll be nineteen next week."

He moved away from the bag to address the five of us.

"Congratulations for making the choice, not only to commit to getting fit, but also to raising money for such a good cause. I don't know how much you know about the sport, but boxing requires speed, power, mental toughness and agility. We'll work on the basic stance to start with."

After we'd perfected where to put our feet, he gathered us into a huddle. He beckoned me forwards. "You'll help me demonstrate, won't you?" His teeth were perfectly white and straight. "What's your name?"

"Bo," I answered.

A look I recognised crossed his face. I heard someone laugh, so before any stupid jokes, I added quickly, "Yes, *Bo*, like hair BOW."

"Well, Bo," he handed me some pads, smiling, "put these on over your hands. You'll find a space for each finger. Then hold out your hands, palms out, at chest height and I'll run through the punches."

I steeled my feet into the ground, but needn't have worried. He barely tapped the pads. Going easy on me.

"There are four basic punches," he told us. "I'm sure you may have heard of some, but for those of you who haven't, they're called the jab, cross, hook and uppercut."

He flew through demonstrating, before removing his gloves and saying, "Let's swap."

I handed James the pads and eased my gloves on for the first time. They felt heavy, but good. I tried, and failed, to do up the Velcro wrist straps. James did both up for me and I felt my cheeks get hot. "Thanks."

"Now, jab." He held up a pad and I jabbed my right hand.

"When you punch, extending your hand, try to turn your hand out before the punch lands. You'll have more power. Twist from the shoulder and your hips. Exhale as you punch."

I did as he said. And he was right — punching was easier and felt more natural.

"Cross," he said, holding up the other pad for me to hit diagonally. "OK, good. Now, alternate your hands and give me ten, one after the other. Choose power or speed, but don't worry too much about either."

Hitting those pads as hard and fast as I could, I barely heard him say, "Breathe!"

I stopped, breathless. That had felt amazing! My heart was pounding.

James worked his way through helping the other trainees, getting them to do the same, before pairing us up. The girl with glasses introduced herself as Simone. She was very strong.

By the time James came back to me, I'd got the hang of some of the punches. "We've got an odd number of people tonight," he said. "You can partner with me while I teach the hook."

He strapped his pads back on and held them at right angles to his body at hip height.

"This punch can be the most powerful. Coming from a side angle makes it tricky to defend against if your opponent isn't paying attention. Make sure you pivot. Be light and spring off that back foot, don't glue it to the floor — "

I knew that. I'd seen enough boxing, thanks.

"OW!" James jumped back as I gave him my best right hook. I liked this punch even more than the jab.

"You've certainly got power, but you're swinging round like a wild animal! Your feet are all over the place. Take your time." He cracked a grin. "Let's go for ten. Hit the pads as hard as you can. Shouldn't be difficult, right? Women are always angry about something!"

Shocking! I knew he was just kidding but I raised my eyebrow at James for that sexist comment.

Pummelling the pads, I thought:

Take THAT, cancer!

Screw you, death!

This was the best I'd felt in weeks.

CHAPTER 3
PUNCHBAG

Three weeks later I could skip for a minute without stopping. I still couldn't whip the rope like James and some of the others. They did this thing called 'double-unders', where the rope practically vanished because it moved so fast. But I'd added doing some cardio and could manage ten full push-ups now, too. I liked feeling stronger.

On training nights I came home exhausted. Mum was pleased I had something to focus on and even paid for a punchbag that we hung up in the garage.

I hardly had time to think about Dad, or to notice that Mum wasn't around much: off to her pottery- or jewellery-making classes.

*

"I think you're a natural," James said one night. "Your legs are so muscular!" He pointed to the leg I had up on a bench while tying my shoelace.

"You what?" I asked, frowning, not sure I'd heard him right.

"I mean for boxing, your natural build is quite — "

"Chunky?" I snarled. *Really?*

"Solid is what I was going to say. You have to be so careful these days. I never know which compliments get taken the wrong way. I only meant that you're… you know, a good build for boxing. There's power there. Naturally. You've seen Nicola Adams, right?"

I nodded, feeling calmer. James had only ever been supportive and he'd taken time to show me the moves that I found difficult.

He flashed me a brilliant smile. I actually found him quite cute. He was smart and funny. Some guys didn't like strong, independent girls, but James was much more mature than the boys I knew at school.

I was excited about the charity match. It was only three weeks away! Two girls had already dropped out. Lucy said that often happened; that some people thought it was a cool thing to learn, but had no idea how tough it actually was.

I wasn't a very graceful fighter, but I had power. Lucy said I'd probably be fighting Simone, but I needed to up my game because she was fast as well as strong.

After the session ended, I sat on the bench and took the wrapping off my hands. Everyone filed out. Through the window I watched them dash to cars. Mum's evening classes were held on the same nights that I trained, so there was no point expecting her to pick me up.

We hadn't spoken about Dad much. I worried that by mentioning him I'd upset her, and I guess she felt the same. She hadn't even cleared out his wardrobe yet. I'd been the one to remove his medicine from the bathroom cabinet.

"It's belting it down out there," James said.

My house was only a couple of miles away, and the evenings were light enough to walk, but James was right — it was raining buckets.

"Want a lift?" he called, fussing with the door alarm. "You're only on Keeble Avenue, right?"

I must have given him a weird look because he held up his hands.

He laughed. "Sorry, I'm no stalker! I have a good memory and have to organise everyone's membership forms. I remembered your address."

Of course!

"That'd be great, thanks."

After he locked up, I followed him out. We walked across the road to his car. He opened the car door for me which was an old-fashioned move, but sweet. Dad would have approved.

Owning a car seemed very grown up. I suddenly felt self-conscious and clutched my gym bag on my lap, aware that my shorts revealed a lot of bare thigh. I should have got changed, or just jogged home, but refusing a lift seemed silly.

As soon as he'd started the engine, he asked, "How did you get into boxing then?"

"Because of my dad," I said.

"Does he box?" asked James.

"He doesn't…" I hesitated, choosing my words carefully. No one knew me at this gym and I liked that. At school I got pity and worried glances. I was completely fed up with being *the girl whose dad died*, and just wished life could go back to normal.

"He's not around," I added, casually.

"Sorry to hear that," James said, giving a sympathetic smile. "My dad left us too. I was only eleven. I was so angry. Mum suggested exercise as a way to deal with it. I tried karate and judo, but it was boxing that clicked. Mum's always right!"

"My house is down there, on the left," I said as he drove along Keeble Avenue. "Just here is fine."

He pulled over and turned off the engine. The rain hammered on the roof and sounded like it was going to break through. I reached out and pushed down the handle, but the door didn't budge.

"Sorry!" James exclaimed. "Central locking!"
He pressed a button.

I pushed open the car door and swung my gym
bag out into the rain. At the same time, James
leant across the gearstick and put his hand on
my thigh! The heat from his hand was hot and
sticky. Even though I was halfway out, I froze.
My blood ran cold all through my body.

I turned around to look at him. He smiled in a
way which told me he knew exactly what he
was doing. He glanced at my face. I stared at
his hand. Moving his hand further up my leg,
he squeezed slightly. Dropping my bag onto the
pavement, I swung and punched him in the face.

Something hard gave way and crunched under
my knuckles. His nose!

Leaving the door wide open, I grabbed my bag
and ran down my street as fast as I could.

CHAPTER 4
ATTITUDE

I glanced back, hoping James hadn't followed me. Thankfully, the street was deserted.

My hands were shaking so much that I couldn't get my key in the lock. What had I just done?

The house was quiet and dark. Mum was still out. I dropped my bag at the bottom of the stairs and ran up them two at a time.

Panting and shaking, I leant against my bedroom door. I couldn't believe what had happened. Not only had James touched me — *ewww! How dare he?* — but my reaction had been stupid. What would happen now? No way would I ever set foot in that gym again. I never wanted to lay eyes on that creep.

After I'd calmed down, I took a shower and tried to clear my head as the steaming water poured over me. Then I messed about on my laptop, but my mind kept replaying what had happened. What a snake! Had I acted in *any* way to make him think what he'd done was acceptable? God! Had I invited that kind of move? No! What James had done was like a sucker punch, an unfair hit when I was least prepared.

I couldn't sleep.

Tears kept pricking my eyes. All I could picture was his clammy hand on my leg and that entitled look in his eye. The thing that kept me awake was, would he have tried anything else? Could the situation have got worse?

*

The next day, even though I liked Thursdays,
I bunked off school. I packed a change of clothes
in my school bag and hopped off the bus early.

I headed for the rec ground and changed in
the toilets. I spent ages sitting on the swings,
thinking. I kept hearing Dad's voice in my head.
I could have told him what had happened and
he wouldn't have judged. He'd have defended
me, but he wasn't here now was he? He'd
abandoned me by dying! He'd never be here to
protect me ever again.

Remembering that, and the memories of his
funeral, how ill he'd been... the complete
misery of the last few months washed over me.
My tears flowed.

*

Mum didn't notice, that Friday and the following
Monday, that I didn't go to training. I hadn't told
her about James. I didn't want to worry her
because she had enough on her plate.

But she did notice when I received detention three days in a row for swearing at teachers. The school had phoned her about my attitude. They said they were willing to be understanding, but the temper I was showing had to be dealt with. My behaviour was getting worse, not improving.

At school, I viewed every boy as a potential threat and found it difficult to focus. But more than anything, I was furious that by hitting James it meant I couldn't return to boxing. I didn't want to risk seeing him.

At home, I used the punchbag occasionally, but it didn't feel the same. Without the buzz of training with others, and the charity match to aim for, my heart just wasn't in it.

I started to think more and more about Dad. Sometimes I'd find myself looking through his wardrobe on the nights Mum was at her classes. I stayed up late watching Dad's favourite boxing films: *Raging Bull*, *Rocky* and *The Fighter*.

The charity match was two weeks away. I'd missed a week of training and had been ignoring Lucy's texts. Even if I told her the truth, there's no way she'd believe my word over James's. He'd been at Hands of Stone for four years, and me? Less than a month!

*

I put my key in the door and Mum called out, shrilly, "Bo!"

I knew by the tone of her voice that she'd been waiting for me. Now I was in for it. Had the school called again?

Mum was at the kitchen table, her head in her hands. "I've just had a phone call from the police!"

My legs went wobbly. "You *what*?" I sat down.

"You hit someone?"

James's face swam into my head. "He touched me!" I screamed.

And then it all came out.

Mum gave me a gentle lecture, saying I should have told her immediately. She said that there might be charges pressed against me.

"It's complicated because you didn't tell anyone. There's no physical evidence. He, however, has photos proving he has a black eye and a bloody nose!"

He deserved it though!

*

A police officer came to speak to us about the assault. Mum explained about Dad's illness and the toll it had taken, but I'd begged her not to say anything about James. I couldn't face the questions. I didn't want that sort of spotlight on me.

A few days later we heard that, for some reason not explained to us, the charges had been dropped. But I had to attend something called Teen-**R**-age. A four-week course about anger management. Apparently, I needed to learn how to process anger in an acceptable and non-violent way, and this course would help with that.

Yeah, right.

When the officer told me this, my fists were clenched so tight that my fingernails dug in. But I couldn't afford to lose my temper again.

CHAPTER 5
THE BIG FIGHT

"Hi, I'm Bo and sometimes I get... angry."
I felt ridiculous.

Eight of us teenagers sat in a semi-circle in a
run-down community centre with paint flaking
off the walls. Leading the course was Joan, a
grey-haired woman with glasses. She gripped
her clipboard as if her life depended on it.

"It might surprise you but there are different
types of anger," she began. "Inward, outward
and passive."

She peered over her glasses, making sure we
were listening.

"Inward is when anger is directed towards yourself; telling yourself you're unworthy, or useless, or will never find love, for example."

She nodded at each of us.

"That can be very damaging. Believe it or not, as damaging as outward anger. If this anger isn't explored, then unfortunately it can turn into depression or anxiety."

She polished her glasses with the sleeve of her cardigan.

"I'm sure you're familiar with outward anger? This is when you take it out on someone or something else, smashing things up or hitting people."

I looked round, people were nodding. They all looked like they were getting into this.

No way did I want to waste four weeks of my life being here.

"And have you heard the term 'passive aggressive'? This is when you might ignore people, refuse to speak to them, or act deliberately sarcastic or sulky."

We had to pair up and do some role-playing. I hated that kind of thing.

"Can I speak to you?" I asked Joan after the hour was up.

She ushered me into a small room as everyone else filed out. "What's on your mind, Bo?"

"I don't know why I had to come on this course. I don't belong here."

She barely hid her I've-heard-this-all-before expression. I needed to go into more detail.

Why should I be punished when I hadn't done anything wrong? Fury rose inside me like swirling flames. I took a slow, deep breath to try to calm myself. I wanted to hurl a chair across the room.

"I bet loads of people say this, and yes I know it was wrong to lash out. I'm not denying I lost it, but I never told the police why I hit him."

"Are you suggesting there is ever a reason for striking another individual?"

I snapped. "When you're being sexually assaulted there is!"

She looked shocked. "Bo, that's a very serious allegation. Are you saying that's what happened? If so, I will report it to the police straight away."

"I swear on my life."

*

Now that what had happened was out in the open, I called Lucy to say I'd like to re-join the training sessions and was relieved to hear that James had been fired.

I'd kept up my fitness a little. Mum had added me to her tennis club membership and we'd started playing together after school, which had been really nice. She started taking an interest in my boxing, telling me about good nutrition.

Walking back into the gym after two weeks away felt brilliant.

In the changing rooms, two girls I recognised from training, but hadn't spoken to much because they were in another group, came over to me.

The girl I'd once admired wrapping her hands so expertly flung her arms around my neck, pulling me close. "Thank you!"

Awkwardly, I untangled her arms from around my neck. "What's going on?" I asked.

"Thank you for what you did."

The other girl then said, "James tried to kiss me once but I never told anyone."

She continued, "He found excuses to try and touch me, especially when other trainers weren't around. I told him to get his hands off and he said I was imagining things. Claimed he was 'helping' my technique."

I laughed bitterly.

"We overheard him saying you'd quit. Lucy said it was odd you hadn't told her. And then Simone dropped out," the first girl explained.

"We thought it was odd how many girls had dropped out. Lucy said that often happened. But last week I saw Simone in town and she warned me about James. She left because he tried to pin her against a wall! She reported him too and he's under investigation now," added the second girl.

No longer was it just my word against his.

*

Mum and I went door-to-door together around the neighbourhood to raise sponsorship. People were really generous once we explained the money was for a cancer charity and I collected over £700. It felt good to be doing something that would make an actual difference in people's lives.

I knew fighting wouldn't appeal to everyone, but I found it a positive way of getting fit and keeping busy, and of honouring Dad's memory.

On the night of the big fight, I'd chosen a classic Eminem track to walk out to. As the introduction started, I whacked my gloves together and walked along the short platform leading to the ring as my name was announced.

"Fighting in the red corner is Bo Babyface!"

This was really happening!

Mum was in the front row with her mobile out, ready to film everything. My opponent wasn't from our gym and she looked very fit. Although she was heavier, maybe I'd be quicker?

Wearing red felt empowering and energised me. I just needed to remember my training and I'd do alright. I could only do my best.

I was so keyed up that I didn't even hear the referee explaining the rules. Then, before I knew it, the bell went.

Dad once said, while we watched a match, "It always pays to throw the first punch. It's a mind game as much as anything. You've got to frighten your opponent right away."

With that in mind, I lunged forwards. With my most powerful shot, my right hook, I threw the hardest punch I could. It grazed the side of her head. She was probably expecting a jab, from the surprised look in her eyes. I'd definitely caught her off-guard.

She retreated.

"Float like a butterfly!" Mum yelled, above the roar of the crowd.

And that's how I fought for the three rounds. I tried dancing back to catch my breath, then weaving a little and darting forwards to take her by surprise.

Our match was over before I knew it. The cheers were deafening.

I didn't win. It was close, though; almost a split decision.

Through the sweat dripping off my forehead my vision was blurry. But, just for a second, I thought I glimpsed Dad, looking down from the balcony.

His favourite Ali quote flew into my mind: "Don't count the days, make the days count."

I'd certainly done that. And I was positive that, as long as I faced what I was afraid of in life, I could do anything.

THE END

ABOUT
THE AUTHOR

Emma Norry completed an MA in screenwriting at Bournemouth University and a BA in film. She has been writing and publishing short fiction in local writing competitions and magazines for over 15 years. She loves going to the cinema, reading books and playing video games with her two kids.

Helplines and online support

Here are some excellent resources which can explain any difficult questions you might have:

www.victimsupport.org.uk

www.childline.org.uk

www.nspcc.org.uk

www.youngminds.org.uk